J
782.4216
2
KEL
Kellogg, Steven.
Give the dog a bone

Nick-nack paddywhack, give the dog a bone . . .

These boisterous fellows do a lot more than just roll on home! With Steven Kellogg's winning combination of fresh, funny text and hilarious illustrations, this popular nursery rhymes escalates into a slapstick adventure involving cobblers, cats, chickens, sled dogs, and even velociraptors—an ever-increasing number of clever companions that adds up to a most unusual counting book. This irreverent twist on a traditional counting song is a rollicking good time that begs to be shared over and over again.

"Verse and visuals will send readers rolling back to page one to replay this romp repeatedly."
—PUBLISHERS WEEKLY

"Energetic, engaging, and good humored, with colors as warm as toast, Kellogg's pictures are like old friends always welcomed home for a visit and a song."
—BOOKLIST

COUNT ALL THE DOGS!
I saw one chicken.
And I see a VELOCIRAPTOR!

NO DOGS ALLOWED!
GET LOST! GO BACK!
Nick-nack
paddywhack!
We want
our snack!

GIVE THE DOG A BONE

STEVEN KELLOGG

chronicle books · san francisco

First paperback edition published in 2004 by Chronicle Books LLC.

Book design by Judythe Sieck.
Typeset in Kennerly, Windsor, and Bostonian.
The illustrations in this book were rendered using a combination of colored ink, watercolor, acrylic, and colored pencil.
Manufactured in China.
ISBN 978-0-8118-4609-7

The Library of Congress has catalogued the hardcover edition as follows:
Kellogg, Steven.
Give the dog a bone/Steven Kellogg.
p. cm.
Summary: A variation on the familiar song, "This Old Man," in which an increasing number of dogs look for treats.
1. Folk songs, English—Texts. [1. Folk songs. 2. Dogs—Songs and music, 3. Counting.] I. Title.
OZ8.3.K33 Gi 2000
782.42162'21'00268—dc21
00-02503

10 9 8 7 6 5 4 3 2

Chronicle Books LLC
680 Second Street, San Francisco, California 94107

www.chroniclekids.com

This old man, he played ONE,
He played nick-nack on his drum.

Nickity Nackity
Nackity Nickity
Nickity Nackity
Nackity Nickity
Nickity
Nackity
NACK!

Nick-nack paddywhack, give the dog a bone,
This old man went rolling home.

This old man, he played TWO,
He played nick-nack on his shoe.

Nick-nack paddywhack, give the dogs a bone,

This old man went cobbling home.

3

This old man, he played THREE,

Nick-nack-nick and . . .

Up the tree!

Nick-nack paddywhack, give the dogs a bone,

This old man went purring home.

Purr, purr, purr!

4

This old man, he played **FOUR**,
Nick-**KNOCK**, Nick-**KNOCK** on the door.
KNOCK-nack, paddywhack...

Would you like
a **BONE**?

This old man was welcomed home.

5

This old man...

Give me FIVE!

He played nick-nack on the hive.

Hey pooches, dig the jive!

Nick-nack

paddy

WHACK!

Toss the dogs a bone,

This old man hightailed it home.

This old man, he played SIX,
Told the hen to hatch six chicks...

Faster!
FASTER!

Nick-nack paddywhack, took the chickies home,

This old man is a
DISASTER!

Please,
old man,
we want

NO. NO. NO. NO.
NO. NO. NIX!
SIX NOs, paddywhack.
I've played SIX!
a bone.
CHICK-NAPPER!

7

This old man, he played SEVEN,
Soared right up to doggy heaven.

Nick-nack paddywhack, served them all a bone,

Good-bye kisses,

Sailed back home.

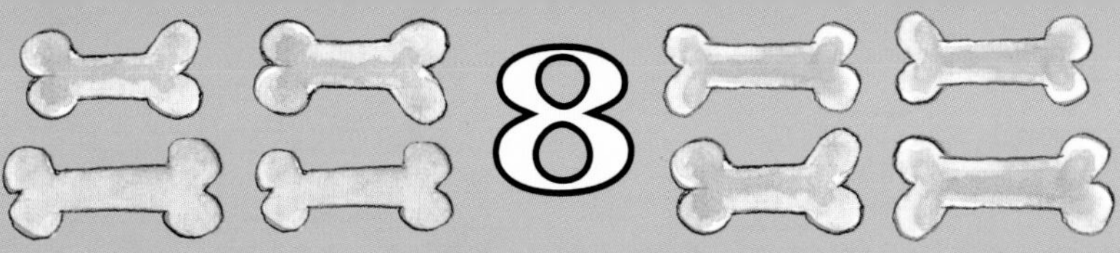

This old man, he played EIGHT,

Past his bedtime,
much too late.

Nick-nack paddywhack

ired and all alone...

Eight kind sled dogs hauled him home.

9

This old man, he played NINE,
Playing nick-nack, feeling fine.

Nick-nack paddywhack, when the ball was thrown,
This old man went sliding home.

OUT!
WE
PICK
NICK
NACK
9
NACK
NACK

WE
BACK
NACK
Yell
"OUT."
BONE
NICK

10

This old man, he played TEN,

Oh, no,
not HIM again.

This time, paddywhack,
TEN eggs, hen!

Nick-nack, shells crack,

Raptors want a bone…

We ten raptors are your captors!

Now we'll tell you what to do:

Give us bones or we'll eat you!

Nick-nack-nickly!
Dogs! COME QUICKLY!

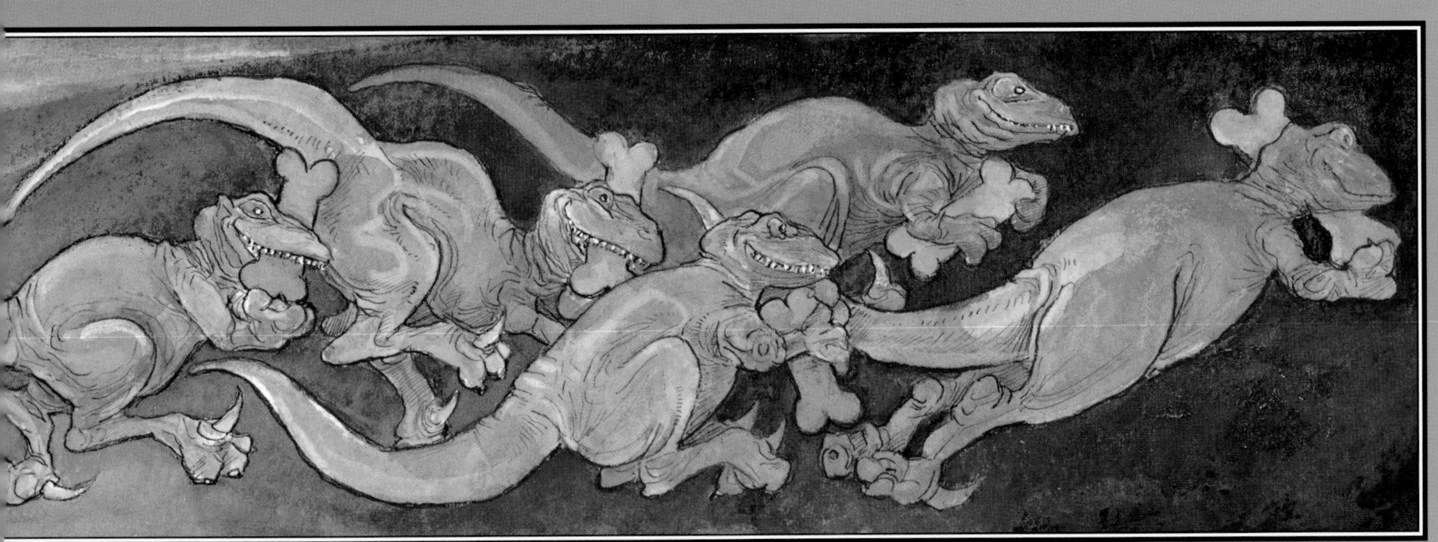

Nick-nack-nick, as our poem ends,
This old man has found some friends.

A NOTE ABOUT THE SONG

This Old Man is a popular nonsense counting song of uncertain origin (perhaps English, perhaps American) that seems to have first appeared in the early twentieth century. Hundreds of variations can be found, since improvisation is often the most entertaining part of any singing game; this version takes off in an entirely original direction after the first verse. Some accompaniments include clapping, stomping, drumming, and motions such as tapping the shoe (for *on my shoe*) or revolving one arm around the other (for *rolling home*). As memorable as it is amusing, portions of this song have been used in joke-telling, pop music, and in the study of speech development. It teaches language, counting, rhythm, and coordination. So . . . *nick-nack paddywack, sing the song below!*

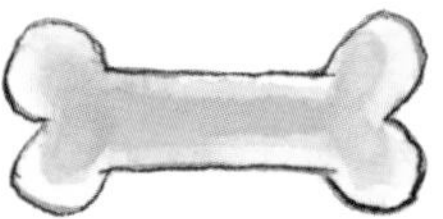

COUNT ALL THE DOGS!

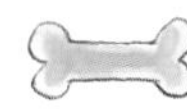

6 Pointers

11 Poodles

19 Rhodesian Ridgebacks

35 Basset Hounds

30 Cairn Terriers

9 English Setters

24 Alaskan Malamutes

33 West Highland White Terriers

4 German Shepherds

32 Great Danes

9 Pugs

25 Golden Retrievers

13 Cocker Spaniels*

*Don't miss Sylvia on the back cover!

STEVEN KELLOGG is the award-winning author and illustrator of over one hundred children's books. One of the most popular author-illustrators working today, he won the Jo Osborne Award for Humor in Children's Literature in 1998. In 1989, the Regina Award acknowledged his distinguished contribution to children's literature. An unabashed dog enthusiast, he lives in Connecticut and upstate New York with his wife, Helen, and his cocker spaniel, Sylvia.